For Ing Hoffman and Anna Burton,
good mothers, good physicians

VIKING
Published by the Penguin Group
Viking Penguin, a division of Penguin Books USA Inc.,
375 Hudson Street, New York, New York 10014, U.S.A.
Penguin Books Ltd, 27 Wrights Lane, London W8 5TZ, England
Penguin Books Australia Ltd, Ringwood, Victoria, Australia
Penguin Books Canada Ltd, 2801 John Street, Markham, Ontario, Canada L3R 1B4
Penguin Books (N.Z.) Ltd, 182-190 Wairau Road, Auckland 10, New Zealand

Penguin Books Ltd, Registered Offices: Harmondsworth, Middlesex, England

3 5 7 9 10 8 6 4 2

Text copyright © Harriet Ziefert, 1989
Illustrations copyright © Suzy Mandel, 1989
All rights reserved
Library of Congress catalog number: 88-82403
ISBN 0-670-82669-3

Printed in Singapore for Harriet Ziefert, Inc.

DR. CAT

Harriet Ziefert
Pictures by Suzy Mandel

VIKING

Ring! Ring!
Ring-a-ling!

Wake up, Dr. Cat!

Dr. Cat went
into the bathroom.

He combed his whiskers.

Then he got dressed.

He put on pants...

a shirt...

a tie...

and a white coat.

Dr. Cat put his bag
on his bike.

He rode to his office.

"Good morning, Dr. Cat,"
said Tim, Jim, and Kim.

"Good morning, Dr. Cat,"
said the nurse.

"Who's first today?"
asked Dr. Cat.

"Not me!" said Tim.
"Not me!" said Jim.
"Not me!" said Kim.

"Somebody has to be first,"
said Dr. Cat.

"Tim and Jim will be first,"
said their mother.

"I'm going to check your ears," said Dr. Cat. "Who's first?"

"You first!" said Tim to Jim.
"You first!" said Jim to Tim.

"I'll be first," said Dr. Cat.

So Tim checked Dr. Cat's right ear.
And Jim checked his left ear.

Then Dr. Cat checked
Tim and Jim.

He checked their ears.
He checked their noses.

"Now I'm going to check throats," said Dr. Cat. "Who's first?"

"You first!" said Tim to Jim.
"You first!" said Jim to Tim.

"I'll be first!" said Dr. Cat.
So Tim and Jim checked Dr. Cat.
"AHH!" said Dr. Cat. "AHH!"

And Dr. Cat checked Tim and Jim.
"Ahhh!" said Tim.

"Ahhhhhh!" said Jim.

"Let me listen first," cried Tim.
"No, me first!" said Jim.

"I'm first," said Dr. Cat.

Dr. Cat listened
to Tim's heart beat.
Ker-thump! Ker-thump!

Then he listened
to Jim's heart beat.
Ker-thump! Ker-thump!

"Give Jim a shot!" said Tim.

"No shots today!" said Dr. Cat.
"But who wants to peek inside
my doctor bag?"

"Me first!" said Tim.
"No, me first!" said Jim.

"They can look together,"
said their mother.

"Good idea!" said Dr. Cat.
"Then you're both first!"